Mel Bay Presents
British & American Victorian Vocal Varieties
By Jerry Silverman

© 1994 BY MEL BAY PUBLICATIONS, INC., PACIFIC, MO 63069.
ALL RIGHTS RESERVED. INTERNATIONAL COPYRIGHT SECURED. B.M.I. MADE AND PRINTED IN U.S.A.

16.95

Contents

British and American Victorian Vocal Varities

ENGLAND

Vivacious Vamps & Vigorous Vagabonds: The Music Hall

Gilbert & Sullivan

AMERICA

Vanished Vows & Vaudeville Virtuosi

Syncopation Rules The Nation

Introduction

On June 20, 1837, William IV of England died. His niece Alexandrina Victoria commenced her reign, which would last until her death 64 years later on January 22, 1901.

King William had said of his niece: "I am sure she will be a good woman and a good queen. It will touch every sailor's heart to have a girl queen to fight for. They'll be tattooing her face on their arms, and I'll be bound they'll all think she was christened after Nelson's ship."

In 1837, Martin Van Buren was President of the United States. Over the next 64 years, seventeen men would occupy that office: William Henry Harrison, John Tyler, James Knox Polk, Zachary Taylor, Millard Fillmore, Franklin Pierce, James Buchanan, Abraham Lincoln, Andrew Johnson, Ulysses Simpson Grant, Rutherford Birchard Hayes, James Abram Garfield, Chester Alan Arthur, Grover Cleveland, Benjamin Harrison, Cleveland for a second time, and William McKinley.

In those 64 years wars were fought, an Empire was built, a nation was torn apart and ultimately saved, steam power and electricity changed the face of the world . . .

These momentous changes are chronicled in the popular songs of that era. Other books in this series, notably, *The American History Songbook, Ballads And Songs Of The Civil War* and *Good Times, Hard Times & Ragtimes* focus in on specific people and events during this period from an American point of view.

Songs Of England, Songs Of Ireland and *Songs Of The British Isles* do the same from an Anglo-Irish perspective.

This present collection looks at popular songs of the Victorian era from a different point of view. There are no momentous changes and earth-shaking events celebrated here. The closest we will come to social commentary is, perhaps, the observation that "a policeman's lot is not a happy one," or the admonition to "shun the poisoned bowl - 'twill lead you down to hell's dark gate, and ruin your own soul."

What we do find here is a rather large dose of sentimentality and pathos intermingled with irreverent humor and lighthearted gaiety, the sparkle of the British music hall, the brilliance of Gilbert and Sullivan, the sweet simplicity of Stephen Foster, the splash of the "Gay Nineties" and the musical apotheosis of the arrival of the 20th century: ragtime, with Scott Joplin and his contemporaries.

The passing of Queen Victoria and the assassination of President McKinley in the same year, 1901, ushered us into the 20th century. The curtain was rung down over an era that had its own point of view—and whose point of view was expressed in its songs every bit as clearly as in the utterances of its leaders and chroniclers. As we approach the turn of a new century, it is important that we preserve and reintroduce to a new audience those songs that meant so much to those citizens of the Victorian era on both sides of the Atlantic.

Elsie From Chelsea

Words and Music by
Harry Dacre

1. Rid - ing one morn - ing, my fare I'd just paid, Oh, what a
2. Said she had no - where par - tic' - lar to go, Oh, what a
3. Went and we supped in a well - known ca - fe, Oh, what a

love - ly day! _____ Gave up my seat to a
love - ly day! _____ Tak - ing the hint, I was
love - ly night! _____ I was bank - rupt be - fore

sweet lit - tle maid, Oh, what a love - ly day! _____
not ve - ry slow, Oh, what a gor - geous day! _____
we came a - way, Oh, what a love - ly night! _____

Tho' she was real - ly a stran - ger to me, Soon in a deep con - ver -
Soon we were gush - ing as lov - ers can gush, Told her I loved her, but
P'raps you will guess that it end - ed in strife, Got a black eye and es -

And Her Golden Hair Was Hanging Down Her Back

Words and Music by
Felix McGlennon

There was once a coun-try maid-en came to Lon-don for a trip, And her
gold-en hair was hang-ing down her back;_____ She was wea-ry of the coun-try, so she
gave her folks the slip; And her gold-en hair was hang-ing down her back._____ It was
once a viv-id au-burn,but her ri-vals called it red, So she thought she would be hap-pier with an

-oth - er shade in - stead; And she stole the wash - ing so - da and ap -

plied it to her head, And some gold - en hair came stream - ing down her

back. _____ But Oh! Flo! such a change you know;

When she left the vil - lage she was shy. _____ But a - las and a - lack!

She's gone back with a naugh-ty lit-tle twin-kle in her eye.

She had a country accent and a captivating glance,
And her golden hair was hanging down her back;
She wore some little diamonds that came from sunny France
And her golden hair was hanging down her back;
She wandered out in London for a breath of ev'ning air,
And strayed into a Palace that was fine and large and fair—
It might be in a Circus or it might be in a Square,
But her golden hair was hanging down her back. *Chorus*

And London people were so nice to artless little Flo,
When her golden hair was hanging down her back;
That she had been persuaded to appear in a tableau
Where her golden hair was hanging down her back;
She posed beside a marble bath upon some marble stairs,
Just like a water nymph or an advertisement for Pears,
And if you ask me to describe the costume that she wears—
Well her golden hair is hanging down her back. *Chorus*

She met a young philanthropist, a friend of Missus Chant,
And her golden hair was hanging down her back;
He lived in Peckham Rye with an extremely maiden aunt
Who had not a hair a–hanging down her back;
The lady looked upon him in her fascinating way,
And what the consequences were, I really cannot say,
But when his worthy maiden aunt remarked his coat next day,
Well, some golden hairs were hanging down the back. *Chorus*

You've Got A Long Way to Go

Words and Music by
A. J. Mills and F. W. Carter

One morn-ing in a lit-tle tail-or's shop I saw dis-played _____ A

pair of la-dies' bloom-ers, sev-en and six-pence,read-y made._____ I

took my daugh-ter in next day, the fel-low got his tape, _____ And

mur-mured as he start-ed put-ting it a-round her shape: _____ "You've

9

got a long way to go, _____ you've got a long way to go; _____

Oh! what a ter-ri-ble lump of stuff, The three-yard meas-ure ain't long e-nough. She's

o-ver nine-ty five _____ 'round her 'se-rag-li-o', _____ To

find a pair of pants to fit her, you've got a long way to go." _____

Once on a donkey's back, I tried Dick Turpin's ride to York,
When suddenly the moke stopped dead and I got off to walk.
'Twas miles out in the country and he wouldn't move for me,
I asked a slop where London was, "Lord luv a duck," said he:

Chorus:
"You've got a long way to go, you've got a long way to go."
He gave the Jerusalem moke a smack,
And planted a pin in its "Union Jack,"
He wouldn't move an inch, the copper said, "What ho!
You'd better get hold of the donkey's rudder, you've got a long way to go."

My wife ain't noted for her looks, her chivvy chase, Oh lor!
It's like a Chinese puzzle or the knocker on the door.
The kids all called her "Monkey Brand" in our localitee,
To find out such a specimen of phi-si-og-no-mee-

Chorus:
"You've got a long way to go, you've got a long way to;
Talk of the girls at the Sandwich Isles
With warts and pimples all round their dials,
I've seen some ugly mugs on view at Barnum's Show,
But to find a face like my old woman's you've got a long way to go.

One day I saw a lady friend a-marching up the West
With such a goody, pious band in blue and scarlet dressed;
She banged upon the tambourine, and shouted to the lot,
"We're marching on to glory!" I said, "Marching on to *What?*"

Chorus:
"You've got a long way to go, you've got a long way to go;
It's no use banging your blooming drum,
And shouting "Sinners, Oh! will you come!"
I like to hear you say you're going to glory, Flo,
If you're only as far as Piccadilly, you've got a long way to go.

Daisy Bell

Words and Music by
Harry Dacre
1892

1. There is a flow-er with - in my heart,
2. We will go "tan-dem" as man and wife,
3. I will stand by you in "wheel" or woe,

Dai - sy, Dai - sy!

Plant-ed one day by a glanc - ing dart,
Ped - 'ling a - way down the road of life
You'll be the bell(e) which I'll ring, you know,

Plant-ed by
I and my
Sweet lit - tle

Dai - sy Bell! _____

Wheth- er she loves me or
When the road's dark we can
You'll take the "lead" in each

loves me not, some-times its hard to tell;_____ Yet I am
both de - spise p'lice-men and "lamps" as well;_____ There are "bright
"trip" we take, then if I don't do well;_____ I will per -

long-ing to share the lot of } beau-ti - ful Dai - sy Bell._____
lights" in the dazz - ling eyes of }
mit you to use the brake my }

Chorus

Dai - sy, Dar - sy, Give me your an - swer, do! _____

I'm half cra - zy, All for the love of you! _____ It won't be a styl - ish mar - riage, _____ I can't af - ford a car - riage. _____ But you'll look sweet on the seat of a bi - cy - cle built for two. _____

Polly Perkins of Paddington Green

Words and Music by
Harry Clifton
1863

I'm a brok-en-heart-ed milk man, in grief I'm ar-rayed, Through keep-ing of the com-pa-ny of a young ser-vant maid, Who liv-ed on board wa-ges, the house to keep clean, In a gen-tle-man's fam'-ly near Pad-ding-ton Green.

Chorus

She was as beau-ti-ful as a but-ter-fly, proud as a queen, Was pret-ty lit-tle Pol-ly Per-kins of Pad-ding-ton Green.

Her eyes were as black as the pips of a pear,
No rose in the garden with her cheeks could compare,
Her hair hung in "ringerlets" so beautiful and long.
I thought that she lov'd me, but found I was wrong.
Chorus

When I'd rattle in a morning, and cry "milk below"
At the sound of my milk cans her face she would show,
With a smile upon her countenance and a laugh in her eye,
If I thought she'd have lov'd me, I'd have laid down to die.
Chorus

When I asked her to marry me, she said, "Oh what stuff"
And told me to "drop it for she'd had quite enough
Of my nonsense" At the same time I'd been very kind.
But to marry a milkman she didn't feel inclin'd.
Chorus

"Oh the man that has me must have silver and gold.
A chariot to ride in, and be handsome and bold;
His hair must be curly as any watchspring.
And his whiskers as big as a brush for clothing."
Chorus

The words that she utter'd went straight thro' my heart,
I sobbed, I sighed, and straight did depart
With a tear on my eyelid as big as a bean,
Bidding good–bye to Polly and Paddington Green.
Chorus

In six months she married, this hard-hearted girl.
But it was not a Wicount, and it was not a Nearl,
It was not a Barronite but a shade or two wus
'Twas a bow legg'd conductor of a twopenny 'bus.
Chorus

Mountains of Mourne

Words and Music by
William Percy French

Oh, Ma - ry, this Lon - don's a won - der-ful sight, With the
don't plant po - ta - toes not bar - ley nor wheat, But there's

peo - ple all work - ing by day and by night. They
gangs of them dig - ging for gold in the

street. At least when I asked them, that's what I was

I believe that when writin', a wish you expressed,
As to how the fine ladies in London was dressed;
Now, if you'll believe me, when asked to a ball,
Faith, they don't wear no tops to their dresses at all.
I've seen them myself, and I would not in troth
Tell if they was bound for a ball or the bath,
Don't be startin' them fashions now, Mary McCree,
Where the Mountains of Mourne sweep down to the sea.

Such beautiful creatures here, och, never mind,
With wonderful shapes nature never designed;
And gorgeous complexions all roses and cream,
But O'Loughlan remarks with regards to them same –
That if at those roses you venture to sip,
The color will all come away on your lip,
So I'll wait for the wild rose that's waitin' for me
Where the Mountains of Mourne sweep down to the sea.

At My Time Of Life

Words and Music by T. W. Connor
c. 1888

1. Now ev - er since I tied the knot, and which it ain't a day, I've
2. I like my drop o' "stim - u - lant" as all good la - dies do A
3. He'd like to see me got up with a cig - a - rette to puff; A

sat - is - fied my hus - band in my good old - fash - ioned way. But since he's seen a
'arf a quart - ern "two out" used to do be - tween the two. But now he says it's
"dick ey dirt" and tie (as if I was - n't guy e - nough!). Says I'd look well in

gal in "bags," it's knocked him sure as fate. He says I ain't worth that be - cause I
on - ly "roughs" as pa - tron - i - zes pubs. For all "new wo - men" wot is "Class," be
bloom - ers and a "call - me - Char - lie" hat! If I'd pro - posed it he'd a said, "Get

① bags - mens pants
② "guy enough"- originally performed by a man in woman's clothes

19

① swagger clubs - women's clubs
② fags - cigarettes
③ certs - sure things (race horses)

The Honeysuckle And The Bee

Words by Albert H. Fitz
Music by William H. Penn

1. On a sum - mer af - ter- noon, Where the hon - ey- suck - les bloom, When all
2. So be - neath the sky so blue, these two lov - ers, fond and true, With their

na - ture seemed at rest,_____ 'Neath a lit - tle rus - tic bow'r, 'Mid the
hearts so filled with bliss,_____ As they sat there side by side, He asked

per - fume of the flow'r, A maid - en sat with one she loved the
her to be his bride, She an - swered, "yes," and sealed it with a

Champagne Charlie

Words Music by Alfred Lee
1868

I've seen a deal of gai-e-ty through-out my nois-y life, With
all my grand ac-com-plish-ments I ne'er could get a wife. The
thing I most ex-cel in is the P. R. F. G. game, A
noise all night, in bed all day, And swim-ming in Cham-pagne.

The way I gained my title's
By a hobby which I've got,
Of never letting others pay,
However long the shot;
Whoever drinks at my expense,
Are treated all the same,
From Dukes and Lords, to cabmen down,
I make them drink Champagne.   *Chorus*

From Coffee and from Supper Rooms,
From Poplar to Pall Mall,
The girls, on seeing me, exclaim,
"Oh, what a Champagne Swell!"
The notion 'tis of everyone,
If 'twere not for my name,
And causing so much to be drunk,
They'd never make Champagne.   *Chorus*

Some epicures like Burgundy,
Hock, Claret, and Moselle,
But Moet's vintage only
Satisfies this Champagne swell.
What matter if to bed I go
Dull head and muddled thick,
A bottle in the morning,
Sets me right then very quick.   *Chorus*

Perhaps you fancy what I say
Is nothing else but chaff,
And only done, like other songs,
To merely raise a laugh.
To prove that I am not in jest,
Each man a bottle of Cham.
I'll stand fizz 'round, yes that I will,
And stand it like a lamb.   *Chorus*

Wot Cher!
Knocked 'Em In The Old Kent Road

Words by Albert Chevalier

Music by Charles Insle
1891

Last week down our al - ley came a toff, Nice old geez-er with a nas-ty cough,
"Ma'am," says he, "I have some news to tell; Your rich un-cle Tom of Cam-ber-well,

Sees my Mis-sus, takes is top-per off, In a ve-ry gen-tle-man-ly
Popped off re, -cent, which it ain't a sell, Leav-ing you 'is lit-tle don-key

way!
shay."

Chorus

"Wot cheer!" all the neigh-bours cried,

"Who're you goin' to meet, Bill? Have you bought the street, Bill?" Laugh! I

27

Thought I should 'ave died.   Knocked 'em in the Old Kent Road!   Road!

Some says nasty things about the moke,
One cove thinks 'is leg is really broke,
That's 'is envy, cos we're carriage folk,
Like the toffs as rides in Rotten Row!
Straight! it woke the alley up a bit
Thought our lodger would 'ave 'ad a fit,
When my missus, who's a real wit,
Says "I 'ates a Bus because it's low!" *Chorus*

When we starts the blessed donkey stops,
He won't move, so out I quickly 'ops,
Pals start whackin' him, when down he drops,
Someone says he wasn't made to go.
Lor it might 'ave been a four in 'and,
My old Dutch knows 'ow to do the grand,
First she bows, and then she waves 'er 'and,
Calling out we're goin' for blow! *Chorus*

Ev'ry evenin' on the stroke of five,
Me and missus takes a little drive,
You'd say, "Wonderful they're still alive,"
If you saw that little donkey go.
I soon showed him that 'e'd have to do,
Just whatever he was wanted to,
Still I shan't forget that rowdy crew,
'Ollerin' "Woa! Steady! Noddy Woa!" *Chorus*

Where Did You Get That Hat?

Words and Music by
Joseph J. Sullivan

1. Now, how I came to get this hat is ve-ry strange and fun-ny: Grand-pa died and left to me his pro-per-ty and mon-ey. And when the will it was read out, they told me straight and flat, If I would have his mon-ey, I must al-ways wear his hat.

2. If I go to the op-'ra house in the op-'ra sea-son, There's some-one sure to shout at me with-out the sligh-est rea-son. If I go to a "Chow-der club," to have a jol-ly spree; There's some-one in the par-ty who is sure to shout at me.

3. At twen-ty one I thought I would to my sweet heart be mar-ried, The peo-ple in the neigh-bor-hood had said too long we'd tar-ried. So off to church we went right quick, de-ter-mined to get wed; I had not long been in there, when the par-son to me said:

The Man Was A Stranger To Me

Words & Music by
T. W. Connor

31

don't think it's go - ing". He said, "Yes, it is," In a tick af - ter that it was
she was good look - ing, so I took the job, And I car - ried it home to her

gone. As I o - pened my eyes, I said, "How the time flies!" My
door. The__ door o - pened wide, and she said, come in - side. Sit

watch in his hand I could see; And I'd a good mind to ask him to
down and I'll make you some tea. You are fond of - pas try?" I

give it me back But the man was a stran - ger to me.
would have said yes, But the girl was a stran - ger to me.

My Fiddle Is My Sweetheart

Words by G. H. Chirgwin
Music by Harry Hunter

"Violin cadenza" ad lib

must have ros - in (rea - son), or will not sing in tune. It's
at the least sug - ges - tion, She'll laugh or she will cry. She'll

not un - til I coax her well that she'll re - veal her charms, But she will sing the
grunt or groan, and sigh or moan, As I wish her to do, And best of all won't

sweet - est song when once she's in my arms. My fid - dle is my sweet - heart, And
speak at all, un - less she's spok - en to. So, lad - ies, there's a won - der, Yes

I'm her faith - ful beau; I take her to my bos - om, Be__ cause I love her so.
won - der - ful but true__ A dam - sel who won't speak at all, Un - less she's spok - en to.

34

I Live In Trafalgar Square

Words and Music by
C.W. Murphy
1902

1. To - day I've been bus - y re - mov - ing,_____ And I'm all of a fidg - et - y fidge;_____ My last digs were on the Em - bank - ment,_____ The third seat from Wa - ter - loo Bridge!_____ But the

2. The beds ain't so soft as they might be,_____ Still, the temp - 'ra - ture's nev - er too high!_____ And, it's nice to see on swells who are the pass - ing,_____ Look on you with en - vi - ous eye,_____ And

3. When I think of those un - luck - y bound - ers,_____ All the Mor - gans and Clar - ence de Clares,_____ Who are forced to put up at the "Ce - cil,"_____ My ten - der - est sym - pa - thy's theirs!_____ And to

Ab7   G

did, and the new place is "ex - tra," I vow! Just
man - y a swell up in Park Lane to - night, Who'd be
soft - head - ed sill - ies won't hear what I say, They

Ab7   G   Am7   Gdim   G7

wait till I tell you where I'm stay - ing now:
glad if he on - ly had my ap - pe - tite
still go on suff - 'ring, while I'm all O. K.

Chorus

C *a tempo*   G7   C   F   Fm

I live in Tra - fal - gar Square, With four li - ons to

C   Em   B7   Em

guard me. Foun - tains and sta - tues all o - ver the

His Lordship Winked at The Counsel

Words by George Dance

Music by Peter Conroy

The Judge took his seat in the court-house one day, A nice Breach of Prom-ise to hear; _____ The Plain-tiff stepped up with a veil 'round her face, A love-ly and blush-ing young dear. _____ She looked at the Ju-ry a sly lov-ing glance, She smiled at the coun-sel be-low; _____ Then

tarn-ing her soft pret-ty eyes to the Judge, She ten-der-ly mur-mured, "Heigh-ho"_____

Chorus

His Lord - ship winked at the Coun - sel, The coun - sel winked at the

clerk; _____ The Ju - ry passed the wink a - long and

mur - mured, "Here's a lark!" _____ The Ush - er winked at the

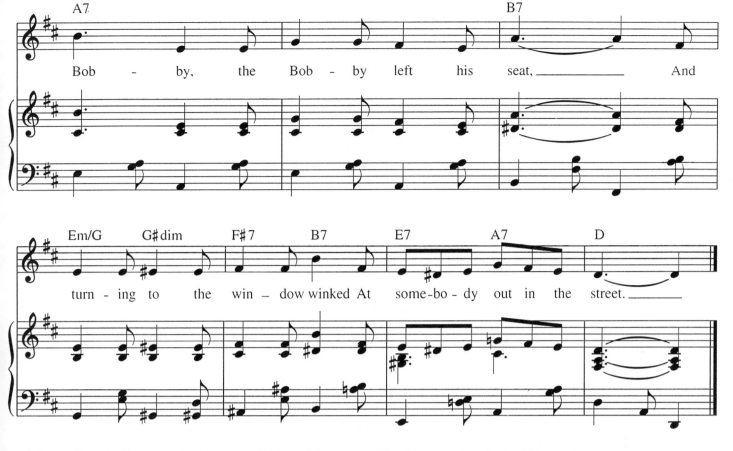

Bob - by, the Bob - by left his seat, _____ And
turn - ing to the win — dow winked At some-bo-dy out in the street. _____

"Pray tell us the facts of your case," the Judge said,
"Your wrongs we are anxious to hear."
"I'll try, my good Lord," the sweet maiden replied,
"My poor heart is broken, I fear.
The monster who wooed me, declared on his oath,
He'd make me his bride by—and—by,
He took me long walks in the moonlight alone
And kissed me when no one was nigh."

Second Chorus:
His Lordship grinned at the Counsel,
The counsel grinned at the Clerk;
The Jury passed a grin along
And murmured, "Here's a lark!"
The Usher grinned at the Bobby,
The Bobby left his seat,
And turning to the window grinned
At somebody out in the street.

The Judge took a pinch of his pungent rappee,
And dignity spread o'er his face.
"You really must name him, my sweet pretty maid,
Or we can't proceed with the case."
The maiden then snatched the thick veil from her cheeks,
And smiled like a mischievous elf;
Then turning around to the Judge cried, "My Lord,
That false—hearted man is yourself."

Third Chorus:
His Lordship blushed at the Counsel,
The counsel blushed at the Clerk;
The Jury passed a blush along
And murmured, "Here's a lark!"
The Usher blushed at the Bobby,
The Bobby left his seat,
And turning to the window blushed
At somebody out in the street.

The Judge viewed the charms of the girl he once loved
And longed her lips once more to press
"Oh sweet pretty maid will you marry me now?
She blushingly answered him, "Yes."
They sent for a parson, they sent for a clerk,
And ere one short hour had sped,
They threw all the fusty law papers aside,
And each held a Prayer Book instead.

Fourth Chorus:
His Lordship tickled the Counsel,
The counsel tickled the Clerk;
The Jury passed a tickle along
And murmured, "Here's a lark!"
The Usher tickled the Bobby,
The Bobby left his seat,
And turning to the window tickled
At somebody out in the street.

The Man Who Broke The Bank At Monte Carlo

Words and Music
by Fred Gilbert
1892

now such lots of mo – ney, I'm a gent._____ Yes, I've
mass of mo – ney, lin – en, silk and starch._____ I'm a
load – stone of my heart What can I do,_____ When with

now such lots of mo – ney, I'm a, gent. _____
mass of mon – ey, lin – en, silk and starch. _____
twen – ty tongues she swears that she'll be true? _____

Chorus

As I walk a – long the *Bois Boo - long,* with an in – de – pen – dent

43

air,_____ you can near the girls de - clare: _____ "He must

be a mil - lion - aire." _____ You can hear them sigh and

wish to die, you can see them wink the oth - er eye at the

man who broke the bank at Mon - te Car - lo. _____

Two Lovely Black Eyes

Words and Music by Charles Coborn
1886

1. Stroll - ing so hap - py down Beth - nal Green,
2. Next time I ar - gued I thought it best, To
3. The mo - ral you've caught, I can hard - ly doubt,

This gay youth you might have seen,
give the Con - ser - va - tive side a rest, The
Nev - er on pol - i - tics rave and shout,

Tomp - kins and I, with his girl be - tween, Oh!
mer - its of Glad - stone I free - ly pressed, When oh!
leave it to oth - ers to fight it out, If

45

A Little Bit Off The Top

Words and Music by
Fred Murray and Alfred Lee

1. Brown's a ve-ry old friend of mine, Once I went to his house to dine;
2. Once I made up my mind to roam, And spend a week by the brin-y foam; I'd

Some of the ar-is-to-cra-cy were there.____
nev-er been far a-way from home be-fore.____

Ev-'ry one of 'em thought me "great," And said, when they saw__ me lick my plate, That
Ev-'ry one of the fam-i-ly were sor-ry in-deed__ to part with me; They

I must be an A - mer - i - can mil - lion - aire. _____ The
all love Wil - lie, es - pe - cial - ly ma - in - law. _____ They

wait - er came in - to the room with a beau - ti - ful lump of pork; ____ And
all came up and asked me for ___ a lock of my gol - den hair; ____ I

though I'd "wolf'd" e - nough to feed a town, _____ I thought I'd like a
clipped 'em from the back and from the side; _____ At last I asked the

sam - ple of the crack - ling and the gra - vy, So I loos - ened out my
mis - sis which par - tic - u - lar bit she fan - cied, And she rubbed her nose and

49

A Motto For Every Man

Words and Harry Clifton
Music by Charles Coote

1. Some peo-ple you've met in your time,— no doubt, Who nev-er look hap-py and gay;— I'll tell you the way to get jol-ly and stout, If you'll lis-ten a-while to my lay.—

2. We can-not all fight in this "Bat-tle of Life," The weak— must go to the wall.— So do to each oth-er the thing that is right, For there's room in this world for us all.— All— "cred-it re-fuse," if you've

bit of my mind And please with the same if I can. _____ Ad –
"mon – ey to pay," You'll find it the much wis – er plan. _____ "A

vice in my song you will cer – tain – ly find, And a mot – to for ev – e – ry
pen – ny lay by for a rain – y day, Is a mot – to for ev – e – ry

man. *Chorus* So we will sing, _____ and _

ban – ish mel – an – cho – ly, Trou –

ble may come, _____ we'll do the best we can, _____ To drive cares a - way, _____ for _ griev - ing is a fol - - ly; "Put your shoul - der to the wheel," is a mot - to for ev 'ry man. _____

A coward gives in at the first repulse,
A brave man struggles again
With a resolute eye and a bounding pulse,
To battle his way amongst men.
For he knows he has one chance in his time,
To better himself if he can.
"So make your hay while the sun doth shine"
That's a motto for every man.   *Chorus*

Economy study but don't be mean,
A penny may lose a pound.
Thro' this world a conscience clean,
Will carry you safe and sound.
It's all very well to be free I will own,
To do a good turn when you can,
But *"Charity always commences at home,"*
That's a motto for every man.   *Chorus*

When I, Good Friends, Was Called To The Bar

In spirited tempo

Gilbert and Sullivan
Trial By Jury
1875

JUDGE

1. When I, good friends, was call'd to the bar, I'd an ap-pe-tite fresh and
2. In West-min-ster Hall I danced a dance, Like a sem-i-de-spond-ent
3. The rich at-tor-ney, he jumped with joy and re-plied to my fond pro-
4. The rich at-tor-ney was good as his word; The briefs came troop-ing
5. At length I be-came as rich as the Gur-neys, An in-cu-bus then I

heart - y, But I was, as man-y young bar-ris-ters are, An
fu - ry; For I thought I nev-er should hit on a chance of ad-
fes - sions: "You shall reap the re-ward of your pluck, my boy, At the
gai - ley, and ev-'ry day my voice was heard at the
thought her, so I threw o-ver that rich at-tor-ney's

im - pe - cu - ni-ous par-ty. I'd a swal-low-tail coat of a
dress - ing a Brit-ish Ju - ry. But I soon got tired of third-class
Bai - ley and Mid-dle-sex Ses - sions. You'll soon get used to her
Ses - sions or An-cient Bai - ley. All those who could my
El - der-ly ug - ly daugh-ter. The rich at-tor-ney my

G ... D7 ... G

beau-ti-ful blue, A ___ brief which I bought of a boo — by, A
jour — neys, And ___ din — ners of bread and ___ wa — ter, So I
looks," said he, "And a ver-y nice girl ___ you'll find her! She may
fees af — ford re — lied on my ___ o — ra — tions, And
cha — rac — ter high tried ___ vain — ly to ___ dis — par — age. And

C ... C#dim ... G ... G#dim ... Am ... F#dim ... G ... C ... D7

cou — ple of shirts and a col — lar or two, And a ring ___ that look'd like a
fell in love with a rich at — tor — ney's El — der — ly, ug — ly
ver — y well pass for for — ty — three, In the dusk, ___ with the light be —
man — y a bur — glar I've re — stored to his friends ___ and his re —
now, if you please, I'm read — y to try this Breach — of — Prom — ise of

G ... CHORUS ... F ... C ... F ... C
f

ru — by! He'd a cou — ple of shirts and a col — lar or two, And a
daugh — ter. So he fell in love with a rich at — tor — ney's ___
hind her!" She may ver — y well pass for for — ty — three, In the
la — tions. And man — y a bur — glar he's re — stored to his
mar — riage. And now, if you please, he's read — y to try this ___

f

I'm Called Little Buttercup

Gilbert and Sullivan
H. M. S. Pinafore
1875

Moderate Waltz tempo

LITTLE BUTTERCUP

I'm called lit – tle But – ter – cup, Dear lit – tle
But – ter – cup, Though I could nev – er tell why; But
still I'm called But – ter – cup, Poor lit – tle But – ter – cup, Sweet lit – tle

59

trea - cle and tof - fee, I've tea and I've cof - fee, Soft
tom - my and suc - cu - lent chops; I've
chick - ens and co - nies, And pret - ty po - lo - nies, And
ex - cel - lent pep - per - mint drops. Then

The Magnet and the Churn

Gilbert and Sullivan
Patience
1881

1. A mag - net hung in a hard - ware shop, And
(2. And) i - ron and steel ex - pressed - sur - prise, The

all a - round was a lov - ing crop of scis - sors and nee - dles,
nee - dles o - pened their well - drilled eyes, The pen - knives felt "shut

nails and knives, Of - fer - ing love for all ___ their ___ loves;
up," no doubt, The scis - sors de - clared them ___ selves "cut ___ out";

65

When All Night Long

Gilbert and Sullivan
Iolanthe
1882

PRIVATE WILLIS

1. When
(2. When)

all night long a chap re - mains On sen - try go, to chase mo -
in that House M. P's di - vide, If they've a brain and cer - e -

not - o - ny He ex - er - cis - es of his brains, That
bel - lum, too, They've got to leave that brain out - side, And

A Policeman's Lot Is Not a Happy One

Gilbert and Sullivan
The Pirates of Penzance
1879

1. When a fell-on's not en-gaged in his em-
2. When the en-ter-pris-ing burg-lar's not a-

ploy-ment (his em-ploy-ment), Or ma-tur-ing his fe-lo-nious lit-tle
burg-ling (not a burg-ling), When the cut-throat is-n't oc-cu-pied in

plans (lit-tle plans), His ca-pac-i-ty for in-no-cent en-
crime ('pied in crime), He ___ loves to hear the lit-tle brook a-

F CHORUS SERGEANT B♭ Gm7 F C7
joy - ment ('cent en - joy - ment) Is just as great as an - y hon - est
gur - gling (brook a gur - gling) And lis - ten to the mer - ry vil - lage
F CHORUS SERGEANT C
man's (hon - est man's) Our feel - ings we with dif - fi - cul - ty
chime (vil lage - chime). When the cos - ter's fin - ised jump - ing on his
G7 CHORUS SERGEANT
smoth - er ('cul - ty smoth - er) When con - stab - u - lar - y du - ty's to be
moth - er (on his moth - er), He loves to lie a - bask - ing in the
C CHORUS SERGEANT
done (to be done).
sun (in the sun).
Ah, take one con - sid - er - a - tion with an

He Is An Englishman

Gilbert and Sullivan
H. M. S. Pinafore
1875

74

Expressive Glances

Gilbert and Sullivan
Princes Ida
1884

Ex - pres - sive glanc - es Shall be our lanc - es, And pops of Sil - le-ry* Our light ar - til - ler-y We'll storm their bow - ers with scent-ed show - ers of fair - est

* Charles Doyne Sillery (1807 – 1837), Irish romantic poet.

sigh). On sweet ur - ban - i - ty, Tho' mere in - an - i - ty, To touch their

FLORIAN

van - i - ty we will re - ly!_____ We'll charm their sens - es With ver - bal

fenc - es, With bal - lads am - a - to - ry And de - clam - a - to - ry. Lit - tle

heed - ing Their pret - ty plead - ing. Our love ex - ceed - ing We'll jus - ti -

fy! Our love ex - ceed - ing We'll jus - ti - fy! _____

CHORUS

_____ Oh, dain - ty tri - o - let! Oh, fra - grant vi - o - let! Oh, gen - tle

heigh o - let! (Or lit - tle sigh). On sweet ur - ban - i - ty, Tho' mere in -

an - i - ty, To touch their van - i - ty We will re - ly! _____

Take A Pair Of Sparkling Eyes

Gilbert and Sullivan
The Gondoliers
1889

Moderately and with warmth

Guitar: capo on 3rd fret; play chords in parentheses.

1. Take a pair of spark - ling eyes, _____ Hid - den, ev – er and a –
2. Take a pret - ty lit - tle cot, _____ Quite a min - ia - ture af –

non, _____ In a mer - ci - ful __ e - clipse. _____ Do not
fair, _____ Hung a - bout with trel - liss'd vine, _____ Fur - nish

heed their mild sur - prise, _____ Hav - ing pass'd the Ru - bi - con. _____ Take a
it up - on the spot _____ With the trea - sures rich and rare _____ I've en-

A Wand'ring Minstrel

Gilbert and Sullivan
The Mikado
1885
NANKI – POO

Slowly, with expression

do so, too, Oh,_____ sor - row, - sor - row! I'll charm your will-ing

ears with songs of lov- ers' fears, While sym-pa - thet-ic tears___ my cheeks be-

dew.____ Oh,_____ sor - row,_ sor - row!

March tempo

But if pa - tri- ot - ic sen - ti - ment is want - ed, I've

86

pa - tri-ot - ic bal - lads cut and dried; For wher-e'er our coun-try's ban - ner may be

plant – ed, All oth – er lo - cal ban-ners are de - fied! Our war - ri-ors, in ser-ried ranks as-

sem - bled, Nev- er quail, or they con-ceal it if they do, And I

should-n't be sur-pris'd if na - tions trem - bled Be-fore the might-y troops, the troops of Ti - ti -

Gracefully, as before

A wan - d'ring min - strel I, A thing of shreds_____ and patch - es, Of bal - lads, songs and snatch - es, And dream - y lull - a - by,_____ And dream - y lull - - a lull - a - by,_____ lull - a - by!

Oh, A Private Buffoon

Guitar : capo on 1st fret;
play chords in parentheses.

Gilbert and Sullivan
The Yeoman Of The Guard
1888

gres - sion, There are one or two rules that all
la - dle; While F is F sharp, and will
mon - ey; He'll ask then and there, with an
sag - es; But should they, by chance, be im -
mon - ey; Bless your heart, they don't mind, they're ex -

fam - i - ly fools Must ob - serve, if they love their pro -
cry with a carp That he's known your best joke from his
in - so - lent stare, "If you know that you're paid to be
port - ed from France, Half - a - crown is stopp'd out of your
ceed - ing - ly kind, They don't blame you, as long as you're

fes - sion! There are one or two rules, Half - a -
cra - dle! When your hu - mour they flout, You can't
fun - ny?" It adds to the task of a
wag - es! It's a gen - er - al rule, Tho' your
fun - ny! It's a com - fort to feel, If your

93

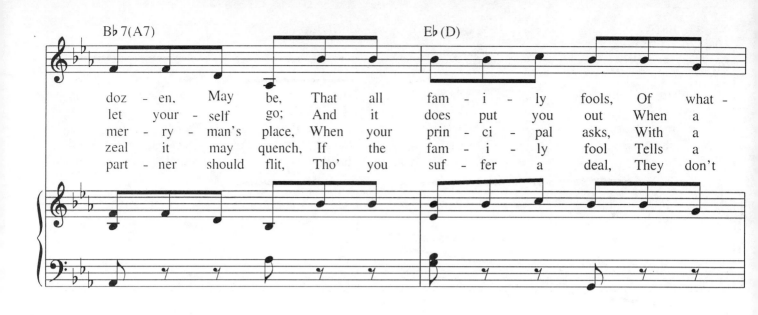

doz - en, May be, That all fam - i - ly fools, Of what -
let your - self go; And it does put you out When a
mer - ry - man's place, When your prin - ci - pal asks, With a
zeal it may quench, If the fam - i - ly fool Tells a
part - ner should flit, Tho' you suf - fer a deal, They don't

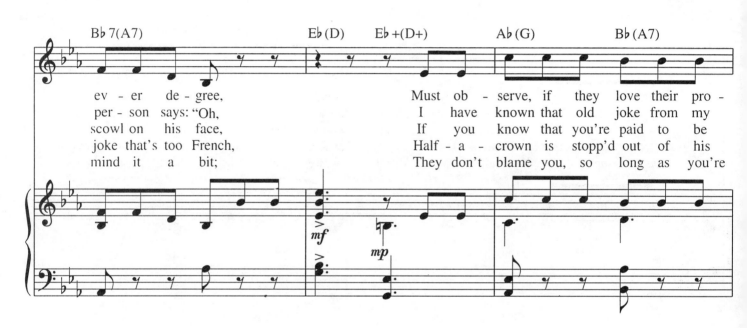

ev - er de - gree, Must ob - serve, if they love their pro -
per - son says: "Oh, I have known that old joke from my
scowl on his face, If you know that you're paid to be
joke that's too French, Half - a - crown is stopp'd out of his
mind it a bit; They don't blame you, so long as you're

fes - sion!
cra - dle!"
fun - ny?
wag - es!

fun - ny!

94

Must I Go Bound?

Must I go bound while you go free? Must I love a lad who don't love me? Must I then, act the child-ish part, And love the lad who'd break my heart?

I put my finger to the bush,
To pluck a rose of fairest kind.
The thorn, it pierced me at a touch,
And oh, I left the rose behind.

Must I go bound while you go free?
Must I love a lad that don't love me?
Was e'er I taught to play the part,
To love the lad who'd break my heart?

Seeing Nellie Home

Words by Francis Kyle

Music by James Fletcher

from Aunt Di - nah's quilt-ing par-ty, I was see - ing Nel - lie home.

On my arm a soft hand rested,
Rested light as ocean foam.
It was from Aunt Dinah's quilting party,
I was seeing Nellie home.   *Chorus*

On my lips a whisper trembled,
Trembled till it dared to come.
It was from Aunt Dinah's quilting party,
I was seeing Nellie home.   *Chorus*

On my life new hopes were dawning,
And those hopes have lived and grown.
It was from Aunt Dinah's quilting party,
I was seeing Nellie home.   *Chorus*

Wait For The Wagon

Words and Music by
R. Bishop Buckley
c. 1850

Will you come with me, my Phil - lis, dear, To yon blue moun-tain free, Where the
ev - ery Sun - day morn-ing when I am by your side, We will

blos-soms smell the sweet-est, Come rove a - long with me. It's ride,
jump in - to the wag-on, And all take a

Wait for the wag - on, Wait for the wag - on,

Wait for the wag - on, And we'll all take a ride.

98

Where the river runs like silver, and the birds they sing so sweet,
I have a cabin, Phillis, and something good to eat.
Come listen to my story, it will relieve my heart,
So jump into the wagon, and off we will start. *Chorus*

Do you believe my Phillis, dear, old Mike with all his wealth,
Can make you half so happy, as I with youth and health?
We'll have a little farm, a horse, a pig and cow;
And you will mind the dairy, while I guide the plough. *Chorus*

Your lips are red as poppies, your hair so slick and neat,
All braided up with dahlias, and hollyhocks so sweet.
It's ev'ry Sunday morning, when I am by your side,
We'll jump into the wagon, and all take a ride. *Chorus*

Together on life's journey, we'll travel till we stop,
And if we have no trouble, we'll reach the happy top,
Then come with me sweet Phillis, my dear, my lovely bride,
We'll jump into the wagon, and all take a ride. *Chorus*

Listen To The Mockingbird

Words and Music by Alice Hawthorne
(Septimus Winner)

grare. Lis-ten to the mock-ing-bird, Lis-ten to the

mock-ing-bird. Still sing-ing where the weep-ing wil-lows wave.

Ah, well I yet can remember, I remember, I remember,
Ah, well I yet can remember
When we gathered in the cotton side by side.
'Twas in the mild mid–September, in September, in September,
'Twas in the mild mid–September
And the mockingbird was singing far and wide. *Chorus*

When charms of spring are awaken, are awaken, are awaken,
When charms of spring are awaken,
And the mockingbird is singing on the bough,
I feel like one so forsaken, so forsaken, so forsaken,
I feel like one so forsaken,
Since my Hallie is no longer with me now.   *Chorus*

Lily Of The West

When I first came to Lou - is-ville, Some pleas-ure there to find, A dam-sel there from Lex-ing - ton was pleas-ing to my mind, Her ros'-y cheeks, Her rub-y lips, Like ar - rows pierced my breast; And the name she bore was

Flo - ra,_____ The Li-ly at the West._____

I courted lovely Flora some pleasure
   there to find,
But she turned unto another man which
   sore distressed my mind.
She robbed me of my liberty, deprived
   me of my rest,
Then go my lovely Flora, the Lily of the West.

I stepped up to my rival, my dagger
   in my hand,
I seized him by the collar and I boldly
   bade him stand.
Being mad to desperation I pierced
   him in the breast,
Then go my lovely Flora, the Lily of the West.

Way down in yonder shady grove, a
   man of high degree,
Conversing with my Flora there, it
   seemed so strange to me.
And the answer that she gave to him
   it sore did me oppress,
I was betrayed by Flora, the Lily of the West.

I had to stand my trial, I had to make
   my plea,
They placed me in a criminal box and
   then commenced on me.
Although she swore my life away,
   deprived me of my rest,
Still I love my faithless Flora, the Lily of the West.

Jeanie With The Light Brown Hair

Words and Music by
Stepher Foster

I dream of Jean - ie with the light brown _ hair, Borne like a va - por
see her trip-ping where the bright streams _ play,
dream of Jean - ie with the light brown _ hair,

on the sum-mer air. I hap-py as the dais - sies that dance on her way.

Man - y were the wild notes her mer - ry voice would pour, Man - y were the blithe birds that

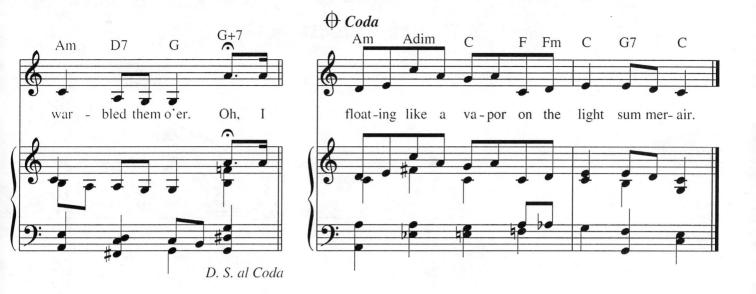

war - bled them o'er. Oh, I

D. S. al Coda

float-ing like a va-por on the light sum mer-air.

I long for Jeanie with the day–dawn smile,
Radiant in gladness, warm with winning guile;
I hear her melodies, like joys gone by,
Sighing round my heart o'er the fond hopes that die;
Sighing like the night wind and sobbing like the rain,
Waiting for the lost one that comes not again;
Ah! I long for Jeanie and my heart bows low,
Never more to find her where the bright waters flow.

Aura Lee

Words by W. W. Fosdick

Music by George R. Poulton
1861

As the black-bird in the spring, neath the wil - low tree,

Sat and piped I heard him sing, Sing of Au - ra Lee.

Au - ra Lee, Au - ra Lee, Maid of gold - en hair;

Sun - shine came a - long with thee. And swal - lows in the air.

106

In thy blush the rose was born;
Music when you spake.
Through thine azure eyes the moon
Sparkling seemed to break.
    Aura Lee, Aura Lee,
    Birds of crimson wing
    Never song have sung to me
    As in that bright, sweet spring.

Aura Lee, the bird may flee,
The willow's golden hair
Swing through winter fitfully,
On the stormy air.
    Yet if thy blue eyes I see,
    Gloom will soon depart.
    For to me, sweet Aura Lee
    Is sunshine through the heart.

When the mistletoe was green
'Midst the winter's snows,
Sunshine in thy face was seen,
Kissing lips of rose.
    Aura Lee, Aura Lee,
    Take my golden ring.
    Love and light return with thee,
    And swallows with the spring.

The Little Orphan Girl

"No___ home, No___ home," Said the lit - tle girl, At the door of a rich man's hall.___ She trem - bl - ing___ stood on the mar - ble steps, And leaned___ on the pol - ished___ wall.___

Her clothes were thin and her feet were bare,
And the snowflakes covered her hair,
"Let me come in," she feebly said,
"Please give me a little bread."

As the little girl still trembling stood,
Before that rich man's door,
With a frowning face he scornfully said,
"No, room, no bread for the poor."

Then the rich man went to his table so fine,
Where he and his family were fed,
And the orphan stood in the snow so deep,
As she cried for a piece of bread.

The rich man slept on his velvet couch,
And he dreamed of his silver and his gold,
While the orphan lay in a bed of snow,
And murmured, "So cold, so cold."

The hours rolled on through the midnight storm,
Rolled on like a funeral bell.
The sleet came down in a blinding sheet
And the drifting snow still fell.

When morning came, the little girl
Still lay at the rich man's door,
But her soul had fled away to its home
Where there's room and bread for the poor.

The Water Is Wide

I put my hand into some soft bush,
Thinking the sweetest flower to find.
The thorn, it stuck me to the bone,
And, oh, I left that flower alone.

Oh, love is handsome and love is fine,
Gay as a jewel when first it's new.
But love grows old and waxes cold,
And fades away like summer dew.

A ship there is and she sails the sea,
She's loaded deep as deep can be.
But not so deep as the love I'm in,
And I know not how to sink or swim.

I leaned my back against a young oak,
Thinking he was a trusty tree.
But first he bended and then he broke,
And thus did my false love to me.

Ben Bolt

Words by Dr. Thomas Dunn

Music by Nelson Kneass

Oh, don't you re-mem-ber sweet Al - ice, Ben Bolt, sweet Al - ice with hair ___ so

brown? She wept with de-light when you gave her a smile, and trem-bled with fear ___ at your

frown. In the old church - yard in the val - ley, Ben Bolt, In a

cor - ner ob - scure and a - lone. They have fit - ted a slab of ___

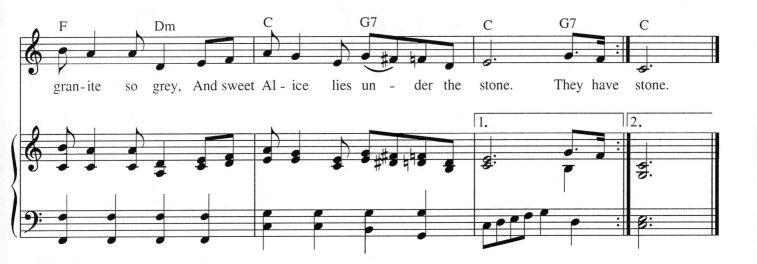

gran-ite so grey, And sweet Al – ice lies un – der the stone. They have stone.

Under the hickory tree, Ben Bolt,
Which stood at the end of the hill,
Together we've lain in the noonday shade
And listen'd to Appleton's mill.
The mill wheel has fallen to pieces, Ben Bolt,
The rafters have tumbled in,
And a quiet that crawls 'round the walls as you gaze,
Has followed the olden din.

And don't you remember the school, Ben Bolt,
With the master so cruel and grim,
And the shaded nook by the running brook,
Where the children went to swim?
Grass grows on the master's grave, Ben Bolt,
The spring of the brook is dry,
And of all the boys who were schoolmates then,
There are only you and I.

The Rose Of Tralee

Words by Mordant Spencer

Music by Charles W. Glover

The pale moon was ris – ing a – bove the green moun-tain, The sun was de –

clin – ing be – neath the blue sea, When I strayed with my love to the

pure crys – tal foun-tain, That stands in the beau – ti – ful vale of Tra – lee.

Chorus

She was love – ly and fair as the rose of __ the __ sum – mer, Yet' 'twas not her

beau - ty a - lone that won me. Oh, no! 'twas the truth in her eye ev - er

dawn - ing, That made me love Ma - ry, the Rose of Tra - lee.

The cool shades of evening, their mantle were spreading,
And Mary, all smiling, was listening to me.
The moon through the valley her pale rays was shedding,
When I won the heart of the Rose of Tralee. *Chorus*

Beautiful Dreamer

Words and Music by
Stephen Foster

Beau-ti-ful dream — er
Sounds of the rude world

wake un-to me, Star-light and dew-drops are wait-ing for thee.
heard in the day Lulled by the moon-light have all passed a-

way. _____ Beau-ti-ful dream — er, queen of my song,

List while I woo thee with soft mel-o-dy. Gone are the cares of

Beautiful dreamer, out on the sea
Mermaids are chanting the wild Lorelei,
Over the streamlet vapors are borne
Waiting to fade at the bright coming morn.
Beautiful dreamer, beam on my heart
E'en as the morn on the streamlet and sea,
Then will all clouds of sorrow depart.
Beautiful dreamer, awake unto me.
Beautiful dreamer, awake unto me.

117

Darling Nellie Gray

Words and Music by
Benjamin R. Hanby
1856

There's a low green _ val-ley by the old Ken-tuck-y shore, Where we've whiled man-y hap-py hours a - way, _____ A _ sit-ting and a - sing-ing by the lit-tle cot-tage door, Where _ lived my _ dar-ling Nel-lie Gray. _____

Chorus Oh, my poor Nel-lie Gray, they have tak-en you a - way, And I'll

One night I went to see her but, "she's gone," the neighbors say.
The white man came and bound her with his chain.
They have taken her to Georgia for to wear her life away,
As she toils in the cotton and the cane. *Chorus*

Sweet Rosie O' Grady

Words and Music by
Maude Nugent

1.Just down a- round the cor- ner of the street where I re - side, There lives the cut-est lit-tle girl that
2.I nev- er shall for- get the day she prom-ised to be mine; As we sat tell-ing love tales in the

I have ev- er spied, Her name is Rose O' Gra-dy and I don't mind tell- ing you, That
gold- en sum- mer time, 'Twas on her fin- ger that I placed a small en- gage-ment ring, While

she's the sweet-est lit- tle rose the gar- den ev - er grew.
in the trees the lit- tle birds this song they seemed to sing!

Chorus

Sweet Ro - sie O' - Gra - dy, My dear lit - tle Rose.

While Strolling Through The Park

Words and Music by
Ed Haley
1884

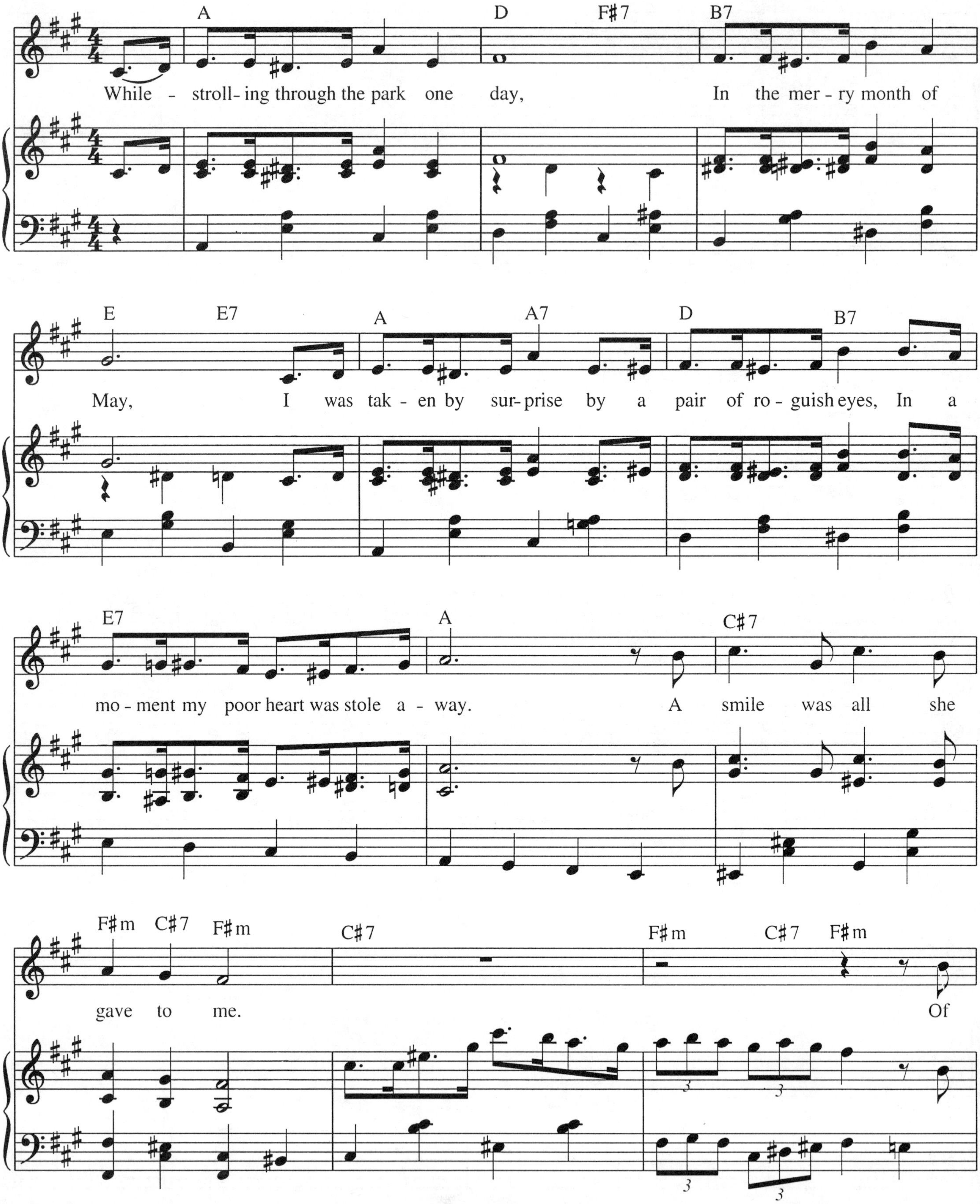
A
D
F#7
B7
While - stroll- ing through the park one day, In the mer - ry month of
E
E7
A
A7
D
B7
May, I was tak - en by sur- prise by a pair of ro - guish eyes, In a
E7
A
C#7
mo - ment my poor heart was stole a - way. A smile was all she
F#m
C#7
F#m
C#7
F#m
C#7
F#m
gave to me. Of

course it made me hap - py as can be.

Ah! I im - me - di - ate - ly raised my hat, And

made a po - lite - re - mark; I nev - er shall for - get the

love - ly af - ter - noon I met her at the foun - tain in the park.

My Sweetheart's The Man In The Moon

Words and Music by
James Thornton

1.Ev - 'ry-bod - y has a sweet-heart un - der - neath the rose,
2.I have of - ten won - der'd where he spends his time all day.

"Ev - 'ry-bod - y loves a bod - y," so the old song goes.
P'raps he has an - oth - er sweet-heart man - y miles a - way.

I've a sweet-heart, you all know him just as well as me.
May - be some sweet dark - hair'd maid - en, dai - ly does he woo.

Ev -'ry eve - ning I can see him short-ly af - ter tea.
But as long as I don't catch him, I'll be - lieve him true.

up   in   a   great   big   bal - loon, _____   And
go - ing   to   mar - ry   next   June, _____   The

see   my   sweet - heart   in   the   moon. _____   Then be -
wed - ding   takes   place   in   the   moon. _____   A

hind   some   dark   cloud   where   no   one   is   al - lowed,   I'll   make
sweet   lit - tle   Ve - nus   we'll   fon - dle   be - tween us,   When   I

love   to   my   man   in   the   moon. _____
wed   my   old   man   in   the   moon. _____

She's Like A Swallow

She's like a swal-low that flies so high, she's like a
riv-er that nev-er runs dry, She's like the sun - shine
on the lee shore; I love my love, __ but love is no more.

Down to this garden this fair maid did go,
To pluck the beautiful prim-a-rose.
The more she plucked, the more she pulled,
Until she got her apron full.

Then out of these prim-a-roses she made
A thorny pillow for her head.
She laid her head down, no word did say,
And then this poor maid's heart did break.

I'll Take You Home Again, Kathleen

Words and Music by
Thomas Wessendorf

D. C. al Coda for Chorus

⊕ Coda

129

I know you love me, Kathleen dear,
Your heart was ever fond and true,
I always feel when you are near,
That life holds nothing, dear, but you.
The smiles that once you gave to me,
I scarcely ever see them now;
Though many times I see
A dark'ning shadow on your brow. *Chorus*

To that dear home beyond the sea,
My Kathleen shall again return,
And when thy old friends welcome thee,
Thy loving heart will cease to yearn.
Where laughs the little silver stream,
Beside your mother's humble cot,
And brightest rays of sunshine gleam,
There all your grief will be forget. *Chorus*

Lorena

Words by Rev. H. D. L. Webster

Music by J. P. Webster
1857

when the sum-mer days_ were nigh; Oh!_ the sun can nev-er dip so

low, _____ A – down af – fec – tion's cloud-less sky.

A hundred months have passed, Lorena,
Since last I held that hand in mine,
And felt the pulse beat fast, Lorena,
Though mine beat faster far than thine.
A hundred months, 'twas flowery May,
When up the hilly slope we climbed,
To watch the dying of the day,
And hear the distant church bells chime.

We loved each other then, Lorena,
More than we ever dared to tell;
And what we might have been, Lorena,
Had but our lovings prospered well
But then, 'tis past, the years are gone,
I'll not call up their shadowy forms;
I'll say to them, "Lost years, sleep on!
Sleep on! nor heed life's pelting storms."

The story of that past, Lorena,
Alas! I care not to repeat,
The hopes that could not last, Lorena,
They lived, but only lived to cheat.
I would not cause e'en one regret
To rankle in your bosom now;
For "If we try, we may forget,"
Were words of thine long years ago.

Yes, these were words of thine, Lorena,
They burn within my memory yet;
They touched some tender chords, Lorena,
Which thrill and tremble with regret.
'Twas not thy woman's heart that spoke;
Thy heart was always true to me:
A duty, stern and pressing, broke
The tie which linked my soul with thee.

It matters little now, Lorena,
The past is in the eternal past;
Our heads will soon lie low, Lorena,
Life's tide is ebbing out so fast.
There is a Future! O, thank God!
Of life this is so small a part!
'Tis dust to dust beneath the sod;
But there, up there, 'tis heart to heart.

Little Annie Rooney

Words and Music by
Michael Nolan

1. A winning way, a pleasant smile,
2. The parlor's small, but neat and clean, And
3. We're been engaged close on a year, The

Dressed so neat, but quite in style; Merry
set with taste so quite seldom seen; And you can
happy time is drawing near. I'll wed the

words your time to while, Has little Annie
bet the household queen, Is little Annie
one I love so dear, My little Annie

Rooney. Ev'ry evening, rain or
Rooney. The fire burns cheerfully and
Rooney. My friends declare I am in

The Band Played On

Words by John F. Palmer

Music by Charles B. Ward

1. Matt Ca - sey formed a so - cial club that beat the town for style, And
2. Such kiss - ing in the cor - ner and such whis - p'ring in the hall, And
3. Now when the dance was o - ver and the band played "Home, Sweet Home," They

hir - ed for a meet - ing place a hall. _____ When
tell - ing tales of love be - hind the stairs. _____ As
played a tune at Ca - sey's own re quest. _____ He

pay - day came a - round each week they greased the floor with wax, And __
Ca - sey was the fa - vor - ite and he that ran the ball, Of __
thanked them ve - ry kind - ly for the fa - vors they had shown, Then he'd

137

hind the man who was their joy and pride.
stayed up - stairs and ex - er - cised his feet.
hap - py Miss - is Ca - sey now for life.

For _____ Ca - sey would waltz with the

straw - ber - ry blonde, And the band played on. _____

_____ He'd glide 'cross the floor with the girl he a - dor'd, and the

The Drunkard's Doom

At dawn of day I saw a man stand by a grog sa-loon. His eyes were sunk, his lips were parched, O, that's the drunk-ard's doom.

His little son stood by his side,
And to his father said,
"Father, mother lies sick at home
And sister cries for bread."

He rose and staggered to the bar
As oft he'd done before,
And to the landlord smilingly said,
"Just fill me one glass more."

The cup was filled at his command,
He drank of the poisoned bowl,
He drank, while wife and children starved,
And ruined his own soul.

A year had passed, I went that way,
A hearse stood at the door;
I paused to ask, and one replied,
"The drunkard is no more."

I saw the hearse move slowly on,
No wife nor child was there;
They too had flown to heaven's bright home
And left a world of care.

Now, all young men, a warning take,
And shun the poisoned bowl;
"Twill lead you down to hell's dark gate,
And ruin your own soul."

Home, Sweet Home

Words by John Howard Payn

Music by Henry Rowley Bishop
1823

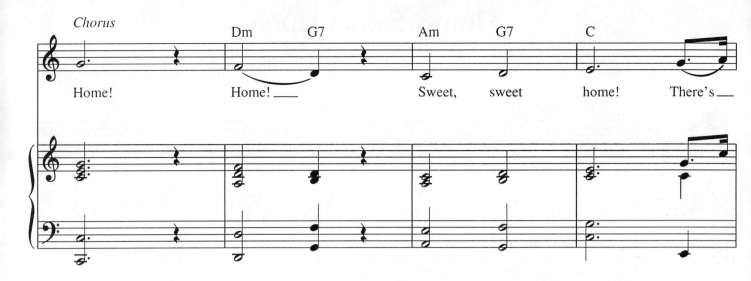

Chorus

| Dm | G7 | Am | G7 | C |

Home! Home! ___ Sweet, sweet home! There's ___

| F | C | A7 | Dm | G7 | C |

no place like home, ___ There's ___ no ___ place like home.

An exile from home, splendor dazzles in vain,
Oh, give me my lowly thatched cottage again.
The birds singing gaily, that come at my call;
Give me them, with that peace of mind, dearer than all. *Chorus*

To thee, I'll return overburdened with care,
The heart's dearest solace will smile on me there.
No more from that cottage again will I roam,
Be it ever so humble, there's no place like home. *Chorus*

Grandfather's Clock

Words and Music by
Henry Clay Work

143

years with-out slum-ber-ing- tick, tock, tick, tock, His life's sec-onds num-ber-ing- tick, tock, tick, tock, It

stopped short, nev-er to go a-gain, When the old man died.

In watching its pendulum swing to and fro,
Many hours had he spent while a boy;
And in childhood and manhood the clock seemed to know,
And to share both his grief and his joy.
For it struck twenty–four when he entered at the door,
With a blooming and beautiful bride,
But it stopped short, never to go again,
When the old man died. *Chorus*

My grandfather said that of those he could hire,
Not a servant so faithful he found;
For it wasted no time, and had but one desire,
At the close of each week to be wound.
And it kept in its place, not a frown upon its face,
And its hands never hung by its side,
But it stopped short, never to go again,
When the old man died. *Chorus*

It rang an alarm in the dead of the night,
And alarm that for years had been dumb;
And we knew that his spirit was pluming its flight,
That his hour of departure had come.
Still the clock kept the time, with a soft and muffled chime,
As we silently stood by his side,
But it stopped short, never to go again,
When the old man died. *Chorus*

Swanee River

Words and Music by
Stephen Foster

All round the little farm I wandered,
When I was young;
Then many happy days I squandered,
Many the songs I sung.
When I was playing with my brother,
Happy was I;
Oh! take me to my kind old mother
There let me live and die   *Chorus*

One little hut among the bushes,
One that I love,
Still sadly to my mem'ry rushes,
No matter where I rove,
When will I see the bees a-humming
All round the comb?
When will I hear the banjo strumming,
Down in my good old home?   *Chorus*

My Old Kentucky Home

Words and Music by
Stephen Foster

They hunt no more for the possum and the coon,
On meadow, the hill and the shore,
They sing no more by the glimmer of the moon,
On the bench by that old cabin door.
The day goes by like a shadow o'er the heart,
With sorrow where all was delight.
The time has come when the poor folks have to part,
Then my old Kentucky home, good night. *Chorus*

The head must bow and the back will have to bend,
Wherever the poor folks may go.
A few more days and the trouble will end,
In the field where sugar–canes may grow.
A few more days for to tote the weary load,
No matter, 'twill never be light.
A few more days till we totter on the road,
Then my old Kentucky home, good night. *Chorus*

In The Gloaming

Words by A. F. Harrison

Music by Meta Orred

In the gloaming, oh my darling!
Think not bitterly of me!
Though I passed away in silence,
Left you lonely, set you free,
For my heart is crushed with longing,
What had been could never be.
It was best to leave you thus, dear,
Best for you and best for me.

To Coda ⊕

Silver Threads Among The Gold

Words by Eben E. Rexford

Music by Hart Pease Dunks

When your hair is silver white,
And your cheeks no longer bright,
With the roses of the May,
I will kiss your lips and say:
Oh! my darling, mine alone, alone,
You have never older grown,
Yes, my darling, mine alone,
You have never older grown.

Love can never more grow old,
Locks may lose their brown and gold,
Cheeks may fade and hollow grow,
But the hearts that love will know
Never, never, winter's frost and chill,
Summer warmth is in them still;
Never winter's frost and chill,
Summer warmth is in them still.

Love is always young and fair,
What to us is silver hair,
Faded cheeks or steps grown slow,
To the heart that beats below?
Since I kissed you, mine alone, alone,
You have never older grown;
Since I kissed you, mine alone,
You have never older grown.

Love's Old Sweet Song

Words by A. Clifton Bingham

Music by J. L. Molloy

Even today we hear love's song of yore,
Deep in our hearts it dwells forever more,
Footsteps may falter, weary grow the way,
Still we can hear it at the close of day.
So till the end when life's dim shadows fall
Love will be found the sweetest song of all. *Chorus*

Long, Long Ago

Words and Music by
Thomas H. Bayly

Tell me the tales that to me were so dear, Long, long a-go,

Long, long a-go, Sing me the song I de-light-ed to hear,

Long, long a-go, long a-go, Now you are come, All my

grief is re-moved; Let me for-get that so long you have roved.

Let me be-lieve that you love as you loved, Long, long a-go, long a-go.

Do you remember the path where we met,
　　Long, long ago - long, long ago?
Ah yes, you told me you ne'er would forget,
　　Long, long ago - long ago.
Then, to all others, my smile you preferred,
Love, when you spoke gave a charm to each word.
Still my heart treasures the praises I heard,
　　Long, long ago - long ago.

Though by your kindness my fond hopes were raised,
　　Long, long ago - long, long ago.
You by more eloquent lips have been praised,
　　Long, long ago - long ago.
But by long absence your truth has been tried,
Still to your accents I listen with pride,
Blest as I was when I sat by your side,
　　Long, long ago - long ago.

The Parting Glass

fill to me the__ part-ing glass_____ Good__ night, And God__ be__ with you all.

Oh, all the comrades e'er I had,
They're sorry for my going away,
And all the sweethearts e'er I had,
They'd wish me one more day to stay,
But since it falls unto my lot,
That I should rise and you should not,
I'll gently rise and softly call;
Good night, and God be with you all.

If I had money enough to spend,
And leisure time to sit awhile,
There is a fair maid in this town,
Who sorely has my heart beguiled.
Her rosy cheeks and ruby lips,
I'll own she holds my heart enthrall'd
Then fill to me the parting glass -
Good night, and God be with you all.

My Mother's Old Red Shawl

It now lies on the shelf, it is fad – ed and torn, That
Chorus It is use – ful no more, yet I fond – ly a – dore, That

dear old shawl my moth-er wore. 'Tis ____ all that is left for this
dear old shawl my moth-er wore. And through life it shall be a loved

heart to a-dore; To bring to mind those hap-py days of yore.
treas – ure to me, That lit – tle old red shawl my moth – er wore.

Fine

D. C. to Chorus

Oh, my heart often aches will a dull throbbing pain,
When childhood visions come again.
And sadly think of the days that are past,
Too joyous and too beautiful to last.
   Oh, fond, lovely childhood made bright by the smile
   Of one whose love could every care beguile.
   How gladly I'd fly from this world's bitter thrall,
   To seek the heart that throbbed beneath this shawl.   *Chorus*

The Maple Leaf Rag Song

ords by Sidney Brown

Music by Scott Joplin

1. I come from old Vir-gin-ny, From the coun-ty Ac-o-mac. I
2. I dropped in-to the swell-est ball, The great ex-clu-sive It. But my
3. The men were struck with jeal-ous-y, The pis-tols 'gan to flash. But the

have no wealth to speak of, 'rept the clothes up-on my back. I can
face was dead a-gin me, And my trous-ers did-n't fit. But when
la-dies gath-ered round me, For I'd sure-ly made a mash. The

do the coun-try hoe-down, I can buck and wing to show, down, And
Ma-ple Leaf was start-ed, My tim-i-di-ty de-part-ed, I
fin-est belle, she sent a boy to call a coach and pair, We

while I'm in the no - tion, just step back and watch my mo - tion. }
lost my tre - pi - da - tion, you could taste the ad - mi - ra - tion. } Oh, ___
rode a - round a sea - son Till we both were lost to rea - son. }

Refrain

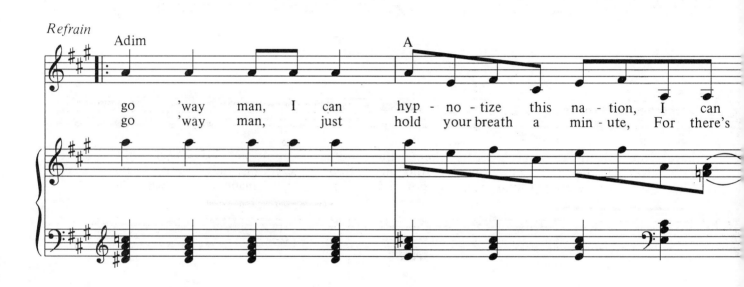

go 'way man, I can hyp - no - tize this na - tion, I can
go 'way man, just hold your breath a min - ute, For there's

shake the earth's foun - da - tion with the Ma - ple Leaf Rag. Oh, ___ Ma - ple Leaf Rag.
not a stunt that's in it with the

The Ragtime Dance Song

Words and Music by
Scott Joplin

I at-tend-ed a ball last Thurs-day night,___ giv-en by the down-town swells. Ev-'ry man came out in full___ dress al-right, And the girls were so-ci-e-ty belles. The

hon-or of be-ing the man-a-ger of the hall. Told the peo-ple to get read-y, for the

time is near at hand, And the dance be-gins at nine o-clock, you know. Then the

or-ches-tra be-gan to play the sweet en-tranc-ing mu-sic of the

most pop-u-lar mel-o-dies of the day. All the cou-ples took their plac-es, All the

men had smil-ing fac-es, While they wait-ed for the call-er to say: Well, ____

Refrain G *a tempo*

Let me see you do the Rag - time Dance, Turn_left and do the cake - walk prance.
Let me see you do the "Clean-up Dance," Now you do the "Jen-nie Cool - er Dance."

G *a tempo*

Turn the oth - er way and do the slow drag. Now you take your la - dy to the

World's Fair; And do the Rag - time Dance. Dance.

At a Georgia Camp Meeting

Words and Music by
Kerry Mills

1. A camp meet-ing took place in a wide o - pen space, 'way down in Geor - gia. There were folks large and small, lan - ky lean, fat and tall At this great
2. The old sis - ters raised sand when they first heard the band, 'way down in Geor - gia. Oh, the preach-er did glare and the dea-cons did stare At the young

Geor-gia camp meet-ing. When church was out how the sis-ters did shout,
peo-ple a - pranc-ing. The band played so sweet that no - bo - dy could eat,

They were so hap - py; But the young folks were ti - red, and
'Twas so en - tranc - ing, So the church folks a - greed it was

wished to be in - spi - red, And hi - red a big brass band.
not a sin - ful deed, And they joined right in with the rest.

Refrain

When the big brass band began to play

I'm Certainly Living a Ragtime Life

Words by Gene Jefferson

Music by Robert S. Roberts

Stood it just ___ as long as I could, ___
Cake - walk mu - sic. it as fills the air, ___

At last I got it and I got it good; ___ First I did - n't want
It can't be dodged be-cause it's ev - 'ry where. Once I did - n't be -

rag - ged time, ___ But now I'm right ___ in line.
long, you see, ___ But now you can't ___ lose me.

Refrain

I got a rag - time dog ___ and a rag - time cat, ___ A rag - time pi - an - o in my

rag - time flat, Wear rag - time clothes from hat to shoes, I read a pa-per called the "Rag - time News." Got rag - time hab-its and I talk that way. I sleep in rag-time and rag all day. Got rag - time trou - bles with my rag - time wife; I'm cer-tain-ly liv - ing a rag - time life.

My Creole Belle

Words and Music by
Sidney and Lampe

All folks are pranc - ing, Sing - ing and danc - ing, Go wild with glee, _____
See them re - hears - ing For this re - joic - ing, That's goin' to be _____

_ I'm as hap - py as hap - py can be, _____ Fill my heart _____ with
_ At the wed - ding 'tween ba - by and me, _____ Oh _ my what _____ a

ec - sta - sy. All o - ver the na - tion, a cel - e - bra - tion
jam - bo - ree. _____ Con - grat - u - la - tions and pre - sen - ta - tions